Patricia Lee Gauch

Poppy's Puppet

ILLUSTRATIONS BY *David Christiana*

HENRY HOLT AND COMPANY

NEW YORK

Henry Holt and Company, Inc., *Publishers since 1866*
115 West 18th Street, New York, New York 10011

Henry Holt is a registered trademark of Henry Holt and Company, Inc.

Published in Canada by Fitzhenry & Whiteside Ltd., 195 Allstate Parkway, Markham, Ontario L3R 4T8.

Library of Congress Cataloging-in-Publication Data
Gauch, Patricia Lee. Poppy's puppet / by Patricia Lee Gauch; illustrated by David Christiana.
Summary: Poppy carves wonderful marionettes from pieces of wood, listening to each piece
to see just what he should make, but when he finds a silent piece
and decides to make it into a ballerina, things do not turn out as planned.
[1. Puppets—Fiction. 2. Toymakers—Fiction. 3. Self-realization—Fiction.] I. Christiana, David, ill. II. Title.
PZ7.G2315Po 1999 [E]—dc21 98-51130

ISBN 0-8050-5291-7 / First Edition—1999
The artist used watercolor on paper to create the illustrations for this book.
Designed by Martha Rago
Printed in the United States of America on acid-free paper.∞
1 3 5 7 9 10 8 6 4 2

For Paul Peabody and his Old Fashioned Marionettes,
particularly Clarinda
—P. L. G.
For Ben and the walking sticks
—D.C.

nce on a narrow lane winding down to the sea, there lived in a tiny house, two rooms high and one room wide, a puppeteer. "Poppy," all the children called him. Their parents did as well.

At first Poppy had simply been a toymaker. The rooms in his home ticked or sang or moved from all the toys that lived in them. A dollhouse as tall as a child sat right in the parlor, and the dolls were forever wondering if it was time for afternoon tea, or who had moved their shoes.

Poppy made every one of the toys himself. He'd find a piece of wood by the side of the road or in someone's rubbish heap, and he'd see—or hear—something in it no one else did.

"It's you, Alice!" he said one day to a piece of oak, and he took it down to the workshop and—whir, whir—he carved Alice in Wonderland. On another day, "It's Toby, isn't it?" he said to a piece of maple, and—whir, whir—the limb became Poppy's dear and forever friendly dog. And so it went.

Poppy the toymaker was happy in his tiny house with its tickings and singing and dolls moving about. But then one day to his surprise, his very own Toby made it clear he wasn't at all happy just barking or being friendly or waiting at Poppy's table for afternoon tea.

At first Poppy couldn't understand what Toby was trying to say. (Dogs and dolls have such whispery voices.) But then, just before he put on his nightcap that night, Poppy exclaimed, "I've got it! You want to be a marionette."

Poppy went down to his workshop, and the whirring started all over again. The treadle went and the spindle turned and, by morning, Toby had knees that bent and legs that moved.

When Poppy finally attached the last string, the dog was already dancing about the workshop.

"What's going on down there?" Poppy's good wife, Jo, called.

That was just the beginning. Now every piece of wood wanted to be a marionette. One cut of an old chestnut turned out to be a leprechaun marionette named Tim with a shoe hammer of his own. A piece of wood—it had been part of a lonely old sycamore by Saint Andrew's Church—became the hedgehog marionette Missus Tiggle Wiggle. Poppy even made a laundry basket for her.

Soon when Poppy sat down to supper—he liked beans with mustard and a touch of rosemary—marionettes of every kind and temperament hung around the walls. And it wasn't long at all before they began to talk to him about their dreams and aspirations.

To a one, they aspired to go onstage.

It was then that Poppy decided to take them on the road. He had a cart and a bicycle; he'd make a traveling show, and he and his marionettes would perform.

Each marionette had a special talent. Toby did great leaping tricks for the show; he'd even leap through a ring of fire. Missus Tiggle Wiggle didn't much like to wash laundry, but she did enjoy going right into an audience of children and collecting their handkerchiefs and such. It was Tim the Shoemaker, though, who proved to be the real hit. Instead of tapping Poppy's shoes with his hammer, he tapped the shoe of each child sitting in the front row. Imagine, a child seeing a leprechaun shoemaker sitting on his or her toe!

As Poppy's success grew and grew, so did his troupe of marionettes. In time, Sinbad the Rabbit, Br'er Elephant the Trickster, and Terebithia the Clown joined the troupe. Poppy always listened to the wood, and he always discovered who and what each marionette wanted to be. Often he would carve and hammer late, late into the night.

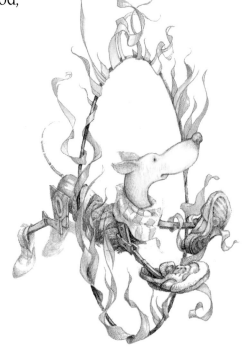

But a terrible thing happened. Clarinda wouldn't dance—not even on the stage. She tripped, falling flat when she did an arabesque. In a pirouette, her strings tangled, her tears ran down her face, and her cheeks ran into her pretty lips as Poppy tried desperately to untangle her strings.

The children laughed.

"Oh dear, oh dear," Poppy said. It was one thing for them to laugh when they were supposed to, when Toby tripped on his tail or the laundry went splat on Missus Tiggle Wiggle's head. But this was to be the high point of the show. Beautiful, not funny!

For many days after that, when Poppy bicycled out to do his show, he left Clarinda hanging on the wall alone. What else could he do?

At suppertime when the marionettes talked about the day's performance, Clarinda was silent.

Then one day—it was a particularly windy spring day, and daffodils had sprung up everywhere, even in the well of Poppy's workshop window—Clarinda fell right off the dining-room wall.

Poppy thought he saw her try to say something. And then he saw her try to move. Without strings! Without ticking! She stood up, slowly, and began to step right along the crack on Poppy's kitchen floor. Tiny foot by tiny foot.

Why, Poppy thought, she's balancing.

Poppy took the scissors and snipped the strings. Snip. Snip. Snip. Her eyelashes fluttered, and for the first time, Poppy was certain he saw her smiling. She stepped along the crack until she met the wall, then collapsed, still smiling.

"Is there something else that I'm to do?" Poppy asked Clarinda. She seemed to be trying to tell him something. But she just sat there, happily. Poppy would have to wait.

The next time Poppy and his troupe went out, Poppy bicycling, his cape flowing, Clarinda rode along. She sat where the other marionettes hung, and from time to time, Poppy would ask her, "What is it, Clarinda? Have you more to show me?" But day after day she only smiled back.

Then one morning—it was certainly June because the roses had begun to twine about the drain spout outside the workshop window—Poppy and the marionettes were rehearsing in the backyard, right under the clothesline.

Clarinda wasn't watching the others as she usually did. Her eyes were, of all things, on the clothesline itself. It was Tim who noticed and tapped on Poppy's shoe to tell him.

At first Poppy couldn't figure out what the tapping was about. "Now stop that, Tim," he said. "We've got work to do." Then the puppeteer looked up at the clothesline and down at Clarinda. Something clicked.

"My goodness," he said, and he said it again right out loud. "My goodness."

He hurried to a pile of branches, picked a rather straight one with a shepherd's crook in it, then fit Clarinda onto the crook so her body stood tall and her legs dangled free, her toes pointed. Her smile was as wide as her cheeks! Never had Poppy seen her smile like that.

Now he lifted her into the air onto the clothesline, and toe by dainty toe, she made her way across the line. She did arabesques back across the wire and in the center a stunning pirouette.

"Ahhhhh," the other marionettes said softly, sounding like the wind itself.

Now Poppy understood. Clarinda had never been a ballerina, not of the usual sort anyway. She was a tightrope dancer and she was wonderful.

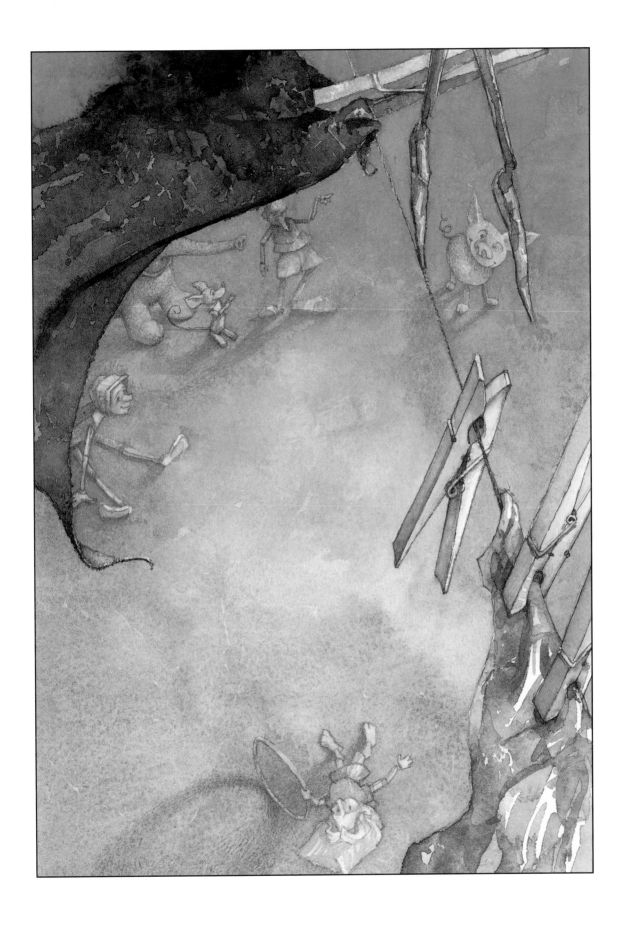

Thereafter Poppy took a wire along just for Clarinda. And after Tim did his tapping and Toby did his newest tricks—he could now slide down a six-foot slide, backward—and after Missus Tiggle Wiggle collected all the laundry from the children and did any dances she intended to do, Clarinda would climb onto the tightrope.

Special, almost mysterious, music from Brazil would play. Silence would settle over the children and their mothers and fathers, and Clarinda would balance and dance across the wire.

"Oh," the children would say as she jumped into the air and landed on one toe on the wire.

"Amazing," others would say as she leaped toe first from one end of the wire to the other.

And when she spun and spun and spun on her dainty toe, right in the middle of the wire, no one could speak at all.

From that day on, on those rare occasions when Poppy found a piece of wood that didn't hum, he would wait in complete silence—even if it was very late or if he was in a great hurry—to hear what it was saying. Never would he shout out "Tailor!" or "Cook!" or "Doctor!" He would listen for the hum in the wood, and in time he knew what the wood wanted to be.

Poppy's family of toys and marionettes grew and grew as did his tiny troupe's fame. The seasons passed. Even after his hair turned gray and, still wearing that same cape, he was hunched over his bicycle handles, Poppy would go to the villages around his village to perform with his troupe. He would pedal up hills and into valleys with his marionettes singing behind him. They rarely whispered anymore. Sometimes they sang duets; sometimes Toby or Tim or Clarinda or one of the new marionettes—and there were always new marionettes—sang a solo.

What never changed was the silence that fell over the audience when Clarinda climbed the tightwire. "Ohhh," they would say as she jumped into the air and landed on one toe. "Amazing," they would say as she leaped the length of the wire. And they would hold their breaths completely as she spun and spun and spun in the middle of the high wire.

The high point, Poppy would whisper to himself, and he never ceased to be amazed.

WITHDRAWN